MW00814081

WHEN IT'S HARD TO TELL THE TRUTH

Gwen Tells Tales

EDWARD T. WELCH

Editor

JOE HOX

Illustrator

Story creation by Jocelyn Flenders, a homeschooling
mother, writer, and editor living in suburban Philadelphia.
A graduate of Lancaster Bible College with a background
in intercultural studies and counseling, the Good News for
Little Hearts series is her first published work for children.

New Growth Press, Greensboro, NC 27404
Text copyright © 2021 by Edward T. Welch
Illustration copyright © 2021 by Joseph Hoksbergen

All rights reserved. No part of this publication may be reproduced, stored
in a retrieval system, or transmitted in any form by any means, electronic,
mechanical, photocopy, recording, or otherwise, without the prior permission
of the publisher, except as provided by USA copyright law.

Unless otherwise indicated, Scripture quotations are taken from the
International Children's Bible® Copyright © 1986, 1988, 1999, 2015 by
Tommy Nelson, a division of Thomas Nelson. Used by permission.

Back Pocket verses (except for 1 John 1:8-9) are taken from the Good News
Translation in Today's English Version- Second Edition Copyright © 1992 by
American Bible Society. Used by Permission.

Cover/Interior Design and Typesetting: Trish Mahoney, themahoney.com
Cover/Interior Illustrations: Joe Hox, joehox.com

ISBN: 978-1-645071-37-2

Library of Congress Cataloging-in-Publication Data on File

Printed in China

28 27 26 25 24 23 22 21   1 2 3 4 5

So you must stop telling lies. Tell each other the truth because we all belong to each other in the same body.

Ephesians 4:25

Gwen Raccoon loved Monday mornings.
She loved them because Monday was the first school day of the week,
and at school Gwen was known as *the* smartest fourth grader
in Mulberry Meadow.

On this Monday morning, as Gwen and her older brother, Gus,
gathered around the breakfast table, Mama made an announcement.

"I hope you both remember that tonight Papa and I have our cornhole game night. We'll be hosting all of the Mulberry Meadow Cornhole Players out back."

Gus rubbed his eyes and asked, "What time will it end?"

Mama set a bowl of berries on the table. "By 9:00, and you should both be in bed by then."

Mama continued,
"And, Gwen, before I forget,
tomorrow's your big math test.
I know Papa's been reminding you to study,
but tonight's your last chance, so
no screens allowed!"

When Gwen heard Mama's words, she let them go in one ear and out the other. She knew she'd pass the test with flying colors. She also wasn't planning to miss any screen time. Especially because Monday evenings were her night to play *Balderdash Bluff* with her friends.

Several of her friends were study animals, but Gwen didn't waste time on such silliness.

BLUFF!

Actually, Miss Minnick often asked *her* to *help* others who were struggling.

Just after supper,
Mama stood in front of the mirror
practicing her game face.

Papa was warming up his throwing arm. Soon their friends would arrive.

"Good luck, Mama!" said Gus. "I'm sure you'll win again.
Maybe this time you will even get a 'four bagger'
and get to sign the board."

Papa exclaimed, "Four bags in the hole in one game?
That would be amazing! She's been practicing nonstop!
This could be the night!"

Mama saw their guests
walking up the path.

"It's show time!"
she shouted,
while racing to the door.
Papa trailed close behind.

Gwen watched through the window until she saw Mama clasp her
favorite cornhole bag. "Perfect!" she whispered and turned toward
the docking station. "Just in time for *Balderdash Bluff*!"

"Hey," said Gus.
"Mama said no screens tonight.
You're supposed to study!"

"Gus, *even* Mama and Papa are playing a game.
Besides, I *always* get As and I *never* study."

"Well, I know *I* need
to study. I have to work
on my science project."

Gwen set an alarm on her tablet
for 8:45, so she'd be in bed before
Mama and Papa were done.
The last thing she wanted
was to get in trouble.

When the alarm buzzed, she quickly
returned her device to the station and
rushed upstairs. She and Gus combed
their fur and brushed their teeth.

"Good luck tomorrow," said Gus.

Gwen set her toothbrush in its cup.

"I don't need luck.
I always get As!"

They peeked out the window and saw
Mama signing the cornhole board!
Everyone was cheering.

Mama had thrown all four bags in the hole!
Now she was the first one on her team to
add her name to the other four-baggers.

"We will never hear the end of this,"
Gus groaned to Gwen as they climbed into bed.

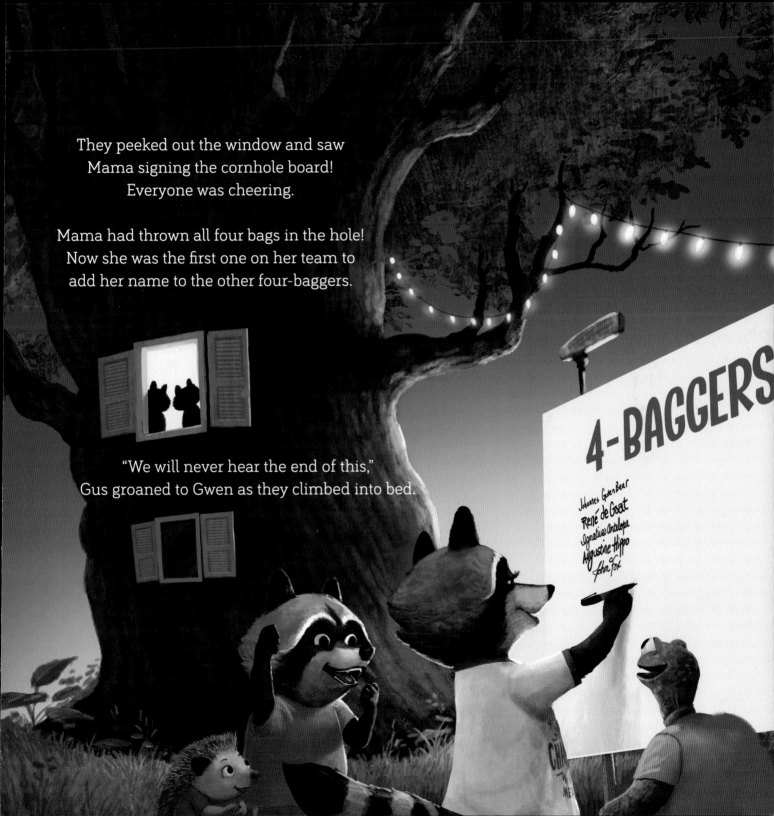

4-BAGGERS

Johannes Gwen Bear
René de Goat
Ignatius Antalope
Augustine Hippo
John Fox

The next morning at breakfast Mama and Papa were still laughing and talking about Mama's amazing win.

"All that practice finally paid off!" said Papa.

Mama just smiled.
Winning felt great.
It was worth all the work.

Papa asked Gwen how she felt about the math test.

"After studying last night, it'll be a piece of cake!" she said.

At school, everything was going perfectly fine until Miss Minnick distributed the tests. Gwen winked at her friends, Tori and Zoe, but when she looked down at the test, she felt completely lost. *Had Miss Minnick ever taught this before? How could she possibly subtract bigger numbers from smaller ones?* She looked around the class—all the other students were feverishly writing—like they knew all the answers.

Oh no,
thought Gwen.

She suddenly remembered that she had been sick for two days last week. Miss Minnick must have taught this while she was home.

Now she really wished she had studied!

At the end of the school day, Miss Minnick returned the tests to the students.
Then, as she often did, she wrote the name of the student with the highest score on the board.
This time it was Henry Hedgehog. The boys roared!

Tori and Zoe rushed to Gwen's side and exclaimed, "What happened? You always get the highest score!" Gwen quickly shoved the test in her backpack and said, "I thought it'd be nice to give someone else a chance for once."

On her way home, she pulled out the test and again read Miss Minnick's words:
Failing Grade. Parent signature required.

Gwen ran the rest of the way home. She burst through the front door and rushed upstairs.
Gus was in his bedroom, finishing up his science project.

Gwen held up her test and groaned,
"Now what am I going to do?
I can't ask Mama to sign this! She'll be so upset,
and she'll know I was online!"

"Whoa!" gasped Gus.
"Maybe you should have studied!"

Gwen quickly realized she'd have
to solve this problem on her own.

Soon she was hiding in the corner
of her room, carefully writing
Mama's signature on her test paper.

At first, Gwen felt relieved.
She wouldn't get in trouble.
She could just forget that she got
an F and next time she would
make a point of studying.

She did feel a little bad for
copying Mama's signature,
but she reminded herself that
it would never happen again.

It wasn't until several days later, when their family ran into Miss Minnick at the market, that things went awry.

"Mrs. Raccoon! I've been meaning to call you!" said Miss Minnick. "How's Gwen been doing since Tuesday's test?"

Gwen had only one plan:
Hide!
She grabbed some large bunches of collard greens and ducked beneath the big leaves.

"She's fine! In fact, she's right . . ." Mama turned around and couldn't find Gwen anywhere. All she saw was a big display of collard greens.

After chatting for a few minutes, Mama looked back and was surprised to see Gwen's purple bow peeking out from the leaves.

"Gwen? Are you hiding?" asked Mama.

As Gwen tried to come out from under the leaves, she realized they'd been wilting and were now sticking to her like glue!

While trying to pry them off, Gwen said,
"Sorry, I was just uh . . . seeing if these were fresh!"

"By wearing them?" asked Mama.

Miss Minnick smiled,
"You must have seen that on *Meadow's
Best Kitchen*! Sometimes I watch that show
and find they have the cleverest ideas! I
especially love how they test all their recipes."

She turned to Mama,
"Speaking of tests, thank you for signing
Gwen's math test this week. I told her I'm available
anytime she needs extra help."

Mama started scooping pecans into her bag and asked,
"*Who* signed her math test?"

UP

Gwen slowly backed away, but Mama's eyes made her stop in her tracks.

Mama kept scooping more and more nuts as Miss Minnick replied,
"*You* did, of course!"

Mama took one final, heaping scoop of nuts.
As she poured them into her bag, it was so full,
that they spilled all over the floor!

"Goodness!" smiled Miss Minnick.
"You must *really* like nuts!"

Mama sealed the bag and said,
"Would you mind if we stopped by Monday
morning before school? That'll give Gwen
and me some time to chat."

"Certainly."

While Mama scampered to collect the nuts
off the floor, their neighbor and friend,
Mrs. Squirrel arrived to gather berries.

She remarked, "Well, if it isn't our new reigning cornhole champion! I'm surprised you're not at home practicing!"

Mama laughed, "Oh, goodness, no! I barely have any time for practicing. My hands are quite full with family and work, and . . . these nuts!"

Gwen looked up surprised; she knew that wasn't true. Mama played cornhole with Papa nearly every night!

As the Raccoon family walked home, Gwen asked, "Mama, why did you lie to Mrs. Squirrel? You said you don't practice, but I see you practicing every day!"

Mama sighed, "I guess I wanted Mrs. Squirrel to think I was just naturally good at cornhole. But you're right, Gwen. That was wrong of me. I'm sorry. I'll straighten things out as soon as we're home.

"And speaking of straightening things out, why don't you explain to us why Miss Minnick thought *I* signed your test?"

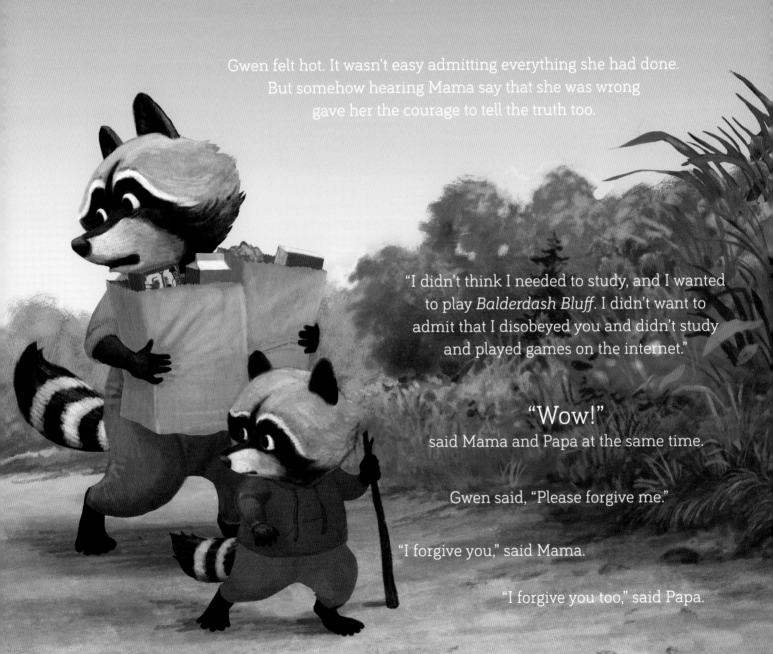

Papa chimed in, "Gwen, you told us
Miss Minnick hadn't returned the tests yet."

Gwen felt hot. It wasn't easy admitting everything she had done.
But somehow hearing Mama say that she was wrong
gave her the courage to tell the truth too.

"I didn't think I needed to study, and I wanted
to play *Balderdash Bluff*. I didn't want to
admit that I disobeyed you and didn't study
and played games on the internet."

"Wow!"
said Mama and Papa at the same time.

Gwen said, "Please forgive me."

"I forgive you," said Mama.

"I forgive you too," said Papa.

Mama said, "You know Gwen, following Jesus
doesn't mean we won't do wrong things."

Papa continued, "But it does mean that when we do,
we ask Jesus for help and forgiveness."

"Sometimes it's hard
to tell the truth,"
Gwen sighed.

"It's easier when we remember
that God will always forgive us
when we ask," said Mama.

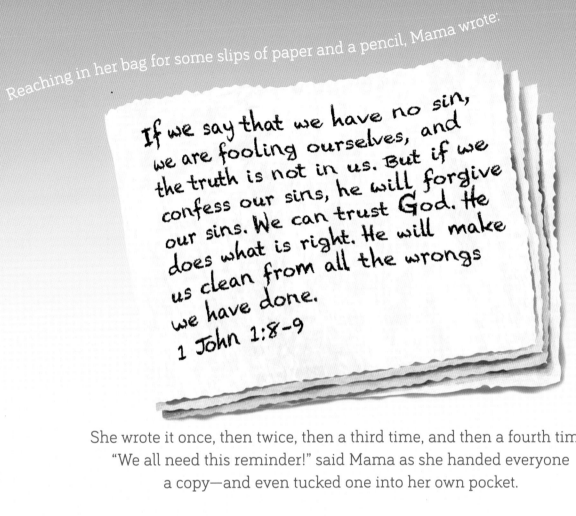

If we say that we have no sin, we are fooling ourselves, and the truth is not in us. But if we confess our sins, he will forgive our sins. We can trust God. He does what is right. He will make us clean from all the wrongs we have done.
1 John 1:8–9

She wrote it once, then twice, then a third time, and then a fourth time.
"We all need this reminder!" said Mama as she handed everyone
a copy—and even tucked one into her own pocket.

Gwen read the words from the Great Book that Mama had written,
and she silently asked Jesus to forgive her.

Then Mama said,
"Now let's get home and eat some of these nuts.
We have enough to last all winter!"

Helping Your Child with Lying

Did you know that honesty and truth telling are part of living a blessed life (Psalm 34:12–13)? But we still lie. Why is that? Often it's because we want to hide something. "I don't want you to see this"—is the logic of most lies. Those who lie usually believe they have done something wrong; or they believe someone will be displeased with what they have done, or both. The wrong might be accidentally jumping into a puddle when wearing good shoes. That is not necessarily wrong, but someone might be upset. Or it could be more serious: the child stole a desired object and does not want to give it up. That's what sin is like: We want something, and we are going to try to get it no matter what God or anyone else says. When we hide, blaming someone else is an easy next step. We are all experts at hiding and blaming.

But our relationship with God and with each other is founded on being trustworthy and honest. God is the truth, so it's impossible for him to lie (Hebrews 6:18). Satan is the liar (John 8:44). When we lie, we believe Satan's lies and imitate his lies. Is there hope? Yes! We can learn to love the truth. Because Jesus came, died, and rose again, we can become truth tellers. In Ephesians, the Apostle Paul introduces our new life this way: "So you must stop telling lies. Tell each other the truth because we all belong to each other in the same body" (Ephesians 4:25). Speaking truth and avoiding lies are a priority for God's people. Lies are divisive. They break our relationship with Jesus and with each other.

You will not eliminate all of your child's lies, but you can form a relationship with your child in which God's words bring truth, the truth is prized, and there are incentives for honesty.

Helping Your Child Walk in the Light

Parents need wise ways to rescue children who lie. This doesn't mean that every lie should be met with a lengthy lecture and Bible study; it does mean that you need a plan.

1   **Develop a relationship in which the truth is welcomed.** To put it another way, don't get angry when children tell the truth about doing something wrong or foolish. An elementary-school-age daughter had been assigned school work, which she was allowed to do online. She knew the family rules about screen time, but she gave in to temptation and went to some of her favorite sites. Later she went to her parents and confessed, "Mom and Dad, when I was supposed to do my homework, I went on other sites." This is a critical moment for parents. You must choose wisely. Since speaking the truth is so important in Scripture, it deserves priority in your conversation. The child has chosen light over darkness, wisdom over foolishness. That gives you a way to say something like this: "What a hard and wise thing! You told the truth rather than tried to hide what you did." This could be followed by some questions and dialogue. For example,

> *"Tell us how you decided to tell the truth."*
> *"How can we help you when you are tempted to disobey?"*
> *"Let's pray. Let's thank Jesus and ask him for help."*

Imagine what would happen if you focused first on the child's disobedience and reacted in anger. Your message would be clear: "Next time, don't make Mommy or Daddy angry, don't speak honestly, cover up those things that provoke." The good news for parents is that missteps and old sins against our children can always be confessed, and children are unusually good at forgiving.

2 **Develop a relationship in which it is natural to confess wrongs.** Parents hope to lead their children away from the bad (deceitfulness and hiding) and into the good (truth-telling and bringing what is hidden to the light), and there are ways you can practice this even when your children are not caught in lies. You can develop your family traditions of confessing sin. "If we say that we have no sin, we are fooling ourselves" (1 John 1:8). Confession is the opposite of lies. It speaks the truth. It comes out into the open, acknowledges wrongdoing, and knows the benefits of forgiveness and restored relationships. As we practice simple confession of sins, we are doing battle with our deceptive instincts.

Prayer before bedtime is a natural place for this, though confession doesn't have to be part of every bedtime ritual—if children have obviously sinned during the day, best that they confess at that time. In the evening, you could say something like this: "Even when we belong to Jesus, we still sin, and God doesn't want us to cover it up. He wants us to confess it, and, of course, he always forgives us. He likes to forgive us (1 John 1:9). Let's pray. I will confess . . . Is there anything you want to confess to Jesus?" Remember that hearing her mother confess that she had lied gave Gwen the courage to confess as well.

Notice how you are not always saying, "Lying is wrong." You are saying that confession is natural and good. Keep Psalm 32:1–5 in mind. It is worth knowing well enough to put in your own words. For example, "We can be really happy when we tell God what we have done wrong—he already knows what we have done, but it is really good for us to say it and ask for forgiveness. When we try to hide what we have done, it can feel like we are carrying around a huge box of junk. After we put it down, we feel so much better. That's what it's like when we tell our

sin to God and know that he forgives us." Speaking like this with your child creates opportunities to talk specifically about the death and resurrection of Jesus for our sins. When Jesus died for our sins, he actually took that box of sins from us.

These two suggestions give you a structure for conversations. Then you work out the details by asking questions. For example, have friends ever lied to your children? What was that like for them? Why do they think we lie? (Like all sin, we lie because we want something that is wrong—and bad for us.) Why do they think God says that lying is wrong? What can we do when we are afraid that we will get in trouble if we tell the truth? As you talk, keep reminding your child that Jesus is right beside them—ready to help them tell the truth and confess their sins when they don't. Jesus will give them the courage and the power to walk in the light (1 John 1:7).